CHAPTER ONE

The streets were wet; the pavements shining and the gutters running over where the drains were clogged with rusty leaves.

Dave was soaked. His overcoat was dripping and underneath that he could feel his jumper and shirt clinging to him with a damp, cold, sticky feel.

He still had about half a mile to walk and knew when he got to the shelter there might be a queue to get in and no free rooms to be had.

He tugged on his rucksack to lift it higher on his sore shoulder. He had stopped thinking. He had ceased to wonder why he was here and how he got himself into this. He gritted his teeth and walked. His hair, which was by now almost down to his shoulders made matters worse. Even his long dark eyelashes were wet and rain getting into his eyes.

The sun was so hot Jade's feet were stinging from the heat as she stepped out of her flip-flops for a moment to ease the sore place between her big toe and the others. She rested her small backpack on a low wall and rubbed the toes, but she had to put the blasted flip-flops back on, because the pavement was like a foretaste of hell. Down the hill she could see the church and as she picked her way over the rounded cobbles, seeking the odd small patches of shadow, she thought she would find out if the church was open. It would be cool in there and she could rest her feet for a while. She threw her hair back and moved the cotton scarf back over it to keep it off her face, to catch any morsel of cooler air that might be blowing. Her pale skin, green eyes and reddish-brown hair made her stand out here, among the swarthy Southern Italians, not that there were any around in this tiny mountainside village.

Beth looked at the white walls, the pale blue curtains and the lino floor. Her iron bed with restraining bars was too high for comfort. She searched for her teddy bear and hugged him with a strange stranglehold. She was not quite sure what she was doing here. She remembered little of the past few weeks. She thought she might be ill. This seemed like a hospital, and she was dressed in a nightgown, but the sun was up and she didn't seem to have a broken leg or anything that should be keeping her in bed. As she moved, a small metal eye on the door clattered shut and a nurse came in with her next sedative injection.

Dave had found a room in the men's hostel, and for now he had it to himself, so he stripped off to his underpants and hung everything on the huge old-fashioned radiator. Thank God for the Victorians, he thought, as steam rose from his soaked clothes. He was under no illusion that someone else would arrive shortly, complain about his wet garments and the steam, and then he'd have to put them back on again, still damp. He had a change of clothes in the rucksack, but despite putting everything in bags, these too were wet through. He grinned to himself as he remembered his mother's predictions: -

'You'll come to no good, my boy, if you carry on like that.' Well, he supposed this was the 'no good'.

Actually, he was very uncomfortable. He was also extremely hungry, but at least he was totally free. He had no commitments, no responsibilities, no job he had to attend, no place of settled abode, and no mortgage. Sadly, he thought 'and no woman'. His mind turned to Jade. He'd met her when he was studying computer science at Manchester, and she was working as a waitress in a pub in the city. She was very young, having left home for a year to 'do her own thing' before applying for Art College. She was a free spirit and fun to be with. She could be ferocious, gentle, teasing and acrobatic. He had never loved her. He didn't really know the meaning of the word. He liked her company. He had glorious sex with her. He missed her when she wasn't around. He knew she had had several partners. He wouldn't call them lovers. She was like him, free and uncomplicated, slightly wild and enjoying a life of experimentation with no ties. She didn't want the ring and the house and the babies, unlike Beth.

Oh dear. The thought of Beth made him feel, for the first time that day, a sense of horrible guilt and foreboding. 'Where was she? Had she had that abortion? Did she still call his name in her nightmares? Where on earth had she landed up? He tried to remember how long it was since she'd been with him. At that time he was living in Sheffield, and sharing a house with an old university mate. He'd done a few jobs, setting up websites for friends. He liked living from hand to mouth. He remembered those rows with Beth: -

'Didn't your parents ever teach you about commitment? I thought they'd been together for over thirty years'

By God they had too. How dull was that.

When he succeeded in getting his 2.1 it was because the subject interested him, not because of the vaguely Victorian work ethic his parents had instilled. He'd had fun as a child playing number games with his dad who taught maths at a local comprehensive. His mum was the practice nurse, and sometimes being an only child, he'd had to accompany her to work where he found books to read, toys to play with and always people to watch. He'd liked to kick a football around on the local rec. at the weekends, but he was basically self-centred and independent.

Now he felt a tug of remorse. He had treated Beth badly. He knew he was the father of that unwanted child. He hadn't known how much Beth wanted it nor how she would react to his suggestion of an abortion. He had pretty much turned on his heel and left her to it when he found out. He shrugged his shoulders and tried to put his mind back on to mundane things like getting his clothes dry. He succeeded to some extent, but his mind kept wandering back to his last few months. 'Damn it' he thought savagely, 'where has this conscience sprung from?'

It was an uncomfortable feeling and one he wasn't used to.

Within minutes the other bed in the room had an occupant. He was a lot older than Dave and a lot dirtier and a lot more worn looking.

'Hi' said Dave and was greeted by a grunt as the tramp settled himself on the bed fully clothed, having parked a newspaper on the duvet cover for his feet, which were still encased in heavy boots. His eyes closed and he disappeared into a snoring heap.

'Ah well, he's not going to bother me' thought Dave and found his way downstairs to the small TV room and got himself some dinner. He tried watching the box, but 'Strictly' wasn't his sort of thing and he had nothing else to do. He wanted to escape the thinking, but it pursued him, relentlessly. Jade and sex. Beth and babies. He picked up an old paperback to read and after re-reading the first paragraph three times put it back on the shelf. At length he went up to the shared room and after a brief wash, put in his earplugs and turned out the light. Even sleep evaded him. He had walked at least twenty miles that day. He was bone tired, and still his mind kept turning.

CHAPTER TWO

Jade found the church at the corner of two incredibly steep streets with a cobbled square in front of it. The whole village looked precipitous as if it would slide down the mountainside at any moment. After cooling her feet on the marble floor, she looked around at the dusty statue of Mary holding the ever-jolly stretching-forward Jesus. He had a chipped plaster nose and painted red cheeks. The flowers were an assortment of tired and faded plastic colours, with the windows too high to clean, buzzing with insects and swathed in drifting cobwebs. An old woman in black was kneeling and muttering her prayers in a pew near the front. Outside there appeared to be no one. It was of course siesta time, but Jade felt as if she were alone on the planet and the old biddy was a dream figure. She hauled out her sketchpad and started a quick pencil sketch of the kneeling figure. Part of her ignored what the old lady was up to, simply drawing the bowed head and wrinkles, and concentrating her efforts on catching a likeness. Part of her was drawn to the stillness of the moment and this strange and foreign idea of a passionate relationship with some invisible being, who never seemed to do anything for anybody she knew, and yet whom millions of people worshipped as if he were real.

She sighed, but the old lady was either deaf or so consumed by her prayers she didn't stop or look up. Jade finished her drawing and went outside. The heat hit her like a wave almost knocking her back into the church. She rummaged around in her bag and found the light scarf to put back on her head. She was looking for her bottle of water when the old lady emerged from the church. She was rather small and very stooped but had a kind face.

'Aqua?' mimed Jade, putting a pretend bottle to her mouth.

'Si Si' replied the woman beckoning Jade to come with her. In spite of her advanced years, she pattered swiftly down the left-hand lane and Jade followed. They reached a tiny, terraced cottage with six enormous steps going up at an angle to the road. Prayer on one's knees must do some good, Jade thought as she followed the speedy old lady into the dark cottage. It was blissfully cool in there and Jade looked longingly at the comfy old chair in the corner. It had a bare wooden table beside it with an old Bible on it.

'Sit. Sit' said the old woman in Italian, beckoning Jade to her chair. Her wrinkles smiled a welcome and Jade sat, drank the water which was offered and accepted gratefully a piece of hard Ciabatta and some cheese. She had forgotten how hungry she was.

The limit of her Italian being 'Grazia' she got to her feet and made to leave, but the old lady stood between her and the door, waving her hand as if to say 'no'. Then she took hold of Jade's wrist in her bony fingers and pulled her towards the stairs. She put both hands under one cheek and tilted her head sideways with her eyes closed. Jade laughed. It was so easy to follow the mime. 'Si.Si. Grazia'

She climbed the steep winding staircase and lay down on the little narrow bed. The woman put a blanket over the bed and proceeded to drape a cool cotton sheet over the top of her. She even placed a small dry kiss on her forehead when she closed her eyes. It was all quite extraordinary, but Jade was too exhausted to argue and immensely appreciative of somewhere comfortable to put her head. She fell into a profound and lengthy sleep.

CHAPTER THREE

Beth woke again, confused with the drugs and the lack of recall as to where she was or why. The nurses who peered through the slot never seemed to come near her. There was a tray of food next to the bed, but she had no memory of anyone bringing it, nor of when it might have arrived. She ate the sandwiches hungrily and found the tea still hot. Surely someone would come to remove the tray and she could ask some questions. She got out of bed and found a dressing gown on the back of a cupboard door. It wasn't hers. Well, she didn't think so. It didn't seem familiar. The slippers were those one-size-fits-all foam things they gave you on aeroplanes. She put them on and tried the door handle. To her surprise it opened. So, she wasn't in a prison then? She took the tray as it gave her an excuse, if she needed one, to be walking down the corridors. She went in search of the kitchens and found a room full of stainless-steel sinks and cupboards and some clean plates, so she attempted to wash up the plate and cup. A voice behind her suddenly said,

'Don't bother with that. It all goes into huge dishwashers - comes out much cleaner than you can get it.'

Beth spun round. The voice came from another inmate, similarly dressed in dressing gown and slippers.

'Hello. I'm Beth. Who are you?'

'Don't rightly know at present. I was Princess Anne yesterday and woke up Zara Phillips this morning. I wish you'd take that monkey off your shoulder. It gives me the creeps'

With that the plump woman walked off and Beth was left with the distinct idea that she'd wandered into a loony bin, but why. Why was she here? What had happened to her?

She continued wandering round till eventually she found an office and someone in a uniform.

'Please can you help me? I need to talk to someone. I need to ask some questions'

'Hello Beth. Yes, you always start with that one. Shall we go into the day room and sit down. I'll get us a cup of coffee and then we'll go through your routines'

'Routines?' thought Beth and wondered if she really was going mad.

'What are these routines?' she asked as they moved swiftly down the corridor, and on into a cheerless day room painted pastel lilac, with faded prints of flowers on the walls.

'Let's start at the beginning, where we always start,' said the white-coated female, 'your name is Beth Turner. You are twenty-three years old. You came in here after a botched abortion attempt. You were a suicide risk and were sectioned for your own safety. You had the baby and then you had severe postnatal depression and rejected it. You signed a paper for it to be adopted and you've been here recovering for the past seven months. You seem to get better and then you relapse, and we have to restrain you or drug you, otherwise you self-harm or become aggressive with the other patients and the staff. We don't have an address for your relatives. You have refused to tell anyone where you live, whether you have parents or any other private details. OK? Does any of that ring a bell?'

'No' said Beth, untruthfully as she recalled her refusal to give any personal details. She did remember she wanted to protect Dave from being harassed by the hospital about her condition, and that she didn't want either of her parents to come marching in, taking over her life again and being self-righteous about her with their 'I told you so' attitude.

'So now I'm better I'd like to leave the hospital. Where are my clothes, please?'

'That's the next bit of conversation we have. You can only leave the hospital if you go with someone who will look after you. You are still in a very fragile condition and since you've talked of suicide, we cannot risk you going out into the community with no back up of any sort. If you would tell us someone we could contact, there might be a chance of release. As it is you need to remain here for the moment.'

Beth sighed, drank her tea and began to plan what she would do. She knew she couldn't contact Dave. If he had ever really loved her, the way she loved him, he wouldn't have ditched her and told her to get an abortion when he found out about the baby.

She couldn't ask her parents to take her. They thought she was happily married in the North of England. She had lied so many times. No wonder she suffered from confusion. At length she said she would go back to her room, but she realised that she had to get out of this place soon. She had to find her baby and get her back.

CHAPTER FOUR

Dave's dream was so real and so startling that he woke confused and with his heart thumping. Jade had definitely been in it and Beth too. There was a moment of sheer terror on a fairground ride where the swinging baskets rising higher and higher had swung out of control and everyone in his world had been flung out sideways. There was a kaleidoscope of broken bodies and souls separating out into a blue-black sky. Dave shuddered and pulled himself up in the narrow bed. The tramp had gone, and Dave looked around for his things. The rucksack had disappeared and his warm overcoat too.

'Damn' he thought. 'I should have slept on those.' He dressed quickly to see if the tramp was still having some breakfast, but he was long gone, and the hostel warden said people's property was their own affair and he couldn't be held responsible. He offered a plastic carrier bag and Dave placed his few remaining bits and pieces in that and set off. His feet were sore, and he had a blister on the back of his left heel. It was drizzling and without his overcoat his clothes soon began to feel uncomfortably damp. As he walked, he started to think all over again about what he was doing and where he was going, not just today but with his life.

He was running out of options. Freedom was all very well, but he needed to eat and sleep, and the thought of his home came back to him. He had always had his own bedroom. He'd had books, warmth, stability, food and as much companionship as he chose. His feet kept moving forward but his mind was elsewhere. If he went abroad at least he'd be warm. A sign to Folkestone appeared on the side of the road and suddenly he was moving towards the possibility of Dover and the continent. He stopped briefly and looked at his watch. He would ring his dad in half an hour and tell him he was alive and well. That was the least he could do, not having been in touch for six weeks at all. Gosh. This conscience thing was extraordinary. Where was it coming from? Maybe it harked back to those Sundays when he was taken unwillingly to Sunday school and dropped off for an hour, so that his parents could have a short respite from him. Certainly, he was fitter than he used to be, after all this daily walking. He was leaner and tougher and had enjoyed the open air, but he began to realise that he needed to settle somewhere for a bit to get a job and make some money, and why not Italy. Jade had said that's where she was heading and although he had no address, he had a sort of fatalistic idea that he might just land up in the same place if he were lucky. He tramped on and decided that he could get to Dover by the next evening.

CHAPTER FIVE

Beth cunningly contrived to find some clothes so she could dress. There was an activity room down one of the corridors and she found a dressing up box in the corner where they used to do plays. 'Role play', she thought, and laughed at the idea of playing a sane human being and not a mad person locked up in a secure ward because she had been sectioned. She knew exactly what she was doing and where she was and why. By keeping herself focussed she had avoided the injections of sleep-inducing drugs. She had stayed calm and knew she was better. She had to get out of here. She knew she was no longer ill, but the doctors were still unwilling to release her into the community without the safeguard of a home to go to and she was determined not to return to her parents. The dressing up clothes had to go on over her nightgown but she had found a long skirt and a shawl, and she had been left with underwear and the foam slippers. One night she had crept along the corridor and worked out where all the doors were. They were mostly locked but you could get into the kitchen and from there through a window out into the grounds. She knew there was a perimeter fence, but she would negotiate that when she got there. The ideas ran faster and more hectically through her mind, as she contemplated the need for money, shelter, clothes and food. All such simple needs, but she'd been hospitalised for weeks and had got used to being looked after.

At least without all those drugs she could think straight. She started to write letters to different agencies and eventually had a reply from a Salvation Army hostel near Dover, who said she could have a room there in exchange for working, maybe in the kitchens. She had told them she was a good cook and able to turn her hand to most menial tasks, making up beds etc. Beth took the letter to the hospital authorities. It appeared she would not have to creep out through a window after all if the Sally Army were willing to sponsor her.

Beth's release from the unit took several days of packing, thinking and meetings with doctors. She knew they would expect her to remain on medication and would want to monitor her progress, but she also knew that she was better, needed no medication and had to find her child and get her back.

A few days later Beth, dressed in her own clothes and looking rather small and scared, left the hospital and made her way to Dover, and the hostel. Although the rooms there were bare and scruffy, Beth didn't mind. She put out her few belongings and settled down quickly to become one of the staff and not just an inmate. There were prayers morning and evening and Beth decided to go. It was something to do and a place to meet the others. After a while she realised this gave her a deep sense of peace and belonging. She sometimes thought of Dave, but instead of resentment and self-pity she started to think of how her love had stifled him and frightened him away. She wondered where he had got to and whether he was happy now or not.

CHAPTER SIX

Meanwhile Jade had completed several drawings in different Italian villages and going on down to Lucca had begun some studies of the walls there.

'Molto bene' came a voice from behind her one morning 'Are you English'

'Yes. How did you guess?'

'Just the way you sit, your clothes, your skin tone, in fact everything about you! Do you want to sell your artwork? I have a stall in the market here on Saturdays. I will sell your paintings if you give me ten per cent of the sales.'

Jade thought hard. She was running out of funds for her travels but was unwilling to part with her paintings. They were to form her portfolio for entrance to Art College next autumn. Maybe she could sign them, take photos and just keep some of the best ones. She had all the rest of the summer and could do more.

'Do you really think they would sell?'

'Si.Si. they are very good. People love local scenes.'

'OK. Thanks.'

'See you on Saturday. Early mind. Six o'clock to set up.'

Off he went and Jade sighed. It was the first human contact she'd had for some time, since the dear old lady had let her sleep on her bed. She'd felt mean leaving there. The old lady had hoped she would stay for a bit, but Jade had to keep moving. She was restless. She enjoyed her drawing and painting and travelling, but sometimes she longed for England and the cool rain and the greenness of it all.

The last sketch of the day took her ages. She wanted to get it absolutely right and it began to get dark as she packed up. As usual she had left finding accommodation until very late. She wandered down into the main square and found a café where she sat and drank coffee and considered her options. The café was pretty full, and a very pretty dark girl came and asked if she could share the table. She also seemed to realise Jade was English and began to talk to her in broken English.

'Ciao. Are you on holiday here?'

'Yes. I'm an art student, trying to travel round Italy and put a portfolio together.'

'May I see?'

'Yes. Help yourself.'

'Wow. These are very good. Why don't you come back to my place and see my drawings? I too am an artist'

'Well. I need to find some cheap accommodation before it gets dark'

'You can stay with me if you like. I have a small flat with a blow-up bed on the floor'

'Are you sure? You don't know me. '

'I like you. You are an artist like me. Come'

The girl picked up the rucksack and put it on her shoulders and grinned broadly at Jade. She had dimples at the sides of her mouth and a wonderful olive coloured skin. She paid for the coffees and led the way across the square and into a tiny medieval back street. They walked for about 10 minutes, barely talking, as the streets were so narrow. Jade followed and watched the slim, dark girl ahead of her with astonishment. Her hair swung from side to side as she walked and she had wonderful anklebones, very slim and suggestive of a great musculature.

Jade wondered if she could draw her. Would it be a cheek to ask? They made their way to the end of a cobbled street and turned left. There, built right into the walls were some tiny medieval houses.

'Here we are. Come up. See where I live.'

Jade climbed up the steep wooden staircase and entered an enchanting room. It was full of stuff. An inflatable double bed, heaped with duvets and cushions, was on the floor near the tiny window, which let in a little light even though it was almost up against the old walls. There was a wooden table, covered in artist's materials and piles of paper and drawings on the floor. In one corner there was a Baby Belling and a few bits of cooking equipment and in another a sink and a tiny toilet behind a curtain.

'It's pretty basic, but I love it here and I go home for a bath occasionally.'

'It's wonderful. Let me see your drawings.'

Jade looked at the sketches in front of her. This girl was obviously quite modern in her approach and did cartoon-like drawings of people and minimalist drawings of buildings, consisting of a few lines here and there.

There seemed nowhere to sit but the double bed on the floor and Jade wondered where she was supposed to sleep. She didn't even know the girl's name. Maybe this was a mistake? But the girl was so pretty and so friendly.

'What is your name by the way? I am Jade'

'I am Rosa. Are you hungry? I make lovely pasta for us'

Jade realised she was indeed ravenous and very tired. She sat down on the bed while Rosa cooked them pasta with a tinned Bolognese sauce. It was delicious and made her feel even sleepier. After they'd eaten Jade started yawning and Rosa said,

'Lie down. Have a sleep.' She helped Jade pull off her shoes and said

'I join you later.'

For a second time Jade found herself on someone else's bed. She yawned, stretched and fell into a deep sleep. When she awoke, she realised that Rosa was curled up on the other side of the mattress facing away from her, but entirely naked.

Jade was shocked but saw an opportunity. She crept up quietly, seized her drawing things and did a beautiful charcoal sketch of Rosa asleep.

The next thing she knew Rosa was awake and giving her that gorgeous grin. She was completely at ease with her own nakedness and wandered round getting breakfast ready for them both. Jade sat watching her and realising with yet more shock that she was finding Rosa incredibly wonderful to watch and that there stirred in her deep desires that she didn't recognise. She had always had plenty of men in her life, but here was a woman she desired just as deeply, and she felt that Rosa was flirting with her and reciprocating those feelings.

CHAPTER SEVEN

Beth had effected the change to the outside world with characteristic determination and grit. She settled quickly to the 'routines', so different from those narrow hospital ones! She thanked God for getting her out of there and began to see that everything that had happened to her might have some purpose. The Salvation Army people were so different from her previous experience. Beth began to look forward each day to being with such kind and friendly people. They were dedicated to practical love. They believed they were God's children, and that included her with all her hang-ups and past mistakes. They were choosing to dedicate their lives to him. Beth wasn't quite of that mindset, but she could see how much happier and more fulfilled they seemed with their lifestyle than she had been with hers so far. She had people she could talk to who were non-judgemental. She became friendly with the hostel manager, called Jenny, and eventually unburdened herself about her baby. Jenny listened and was kind, but when she told Jenny she was determined to find her baby and get her back Jenny asked if she didn't think the baby might be better off in a home where there were two parents and where she was much wanted because the couple hadn't been able to have a child of their own. She suggested that Beth giving up the baby was one of the most unselfish things she'd ever done. There was a lot to think about as she did the cooking, cleaning and domestic chores around the house. She wondered what she should do next, but there wasn't any hurry. They were glad to have her in the home as her cooking really was excellent and there were often so many mouths to feed. Many people who came were far worse off than Beth was, and she began to have a positive and cheerful outlook on life. She had made a firm friendship now with Jenny. Occasionally they would find time to have a cup of tea together and chat. Mainly she was busy and happy and had stopped fretting so much. Little did she know that within days her world would be rocked yet again. Meanwhile she got in touch with the mental hospital and thanked them for looking after her for so long. She even thought of communicating with her parents, but decided she wasn't quite ready for that. When would she ever be? The longer she maintained distance and silence the harder it became. One day Jenny challenged her.

'Do you have any living relatives?'

'Yes,' answered Beth, who couldn't lie to this new friend, 'I still have a mum and dad living near the Peak District.'

'And do they know where you are?'

'No. And I don't want them on my back again.'

'What about their feelings?'

'They told me they never wanted to see me again, so I've kept to that.'

'Ah. We all say things in anger and then regret them. If you are their only child, they must be devastated not to know if you are alive or dead. You could send them a postcard just wishing them well.'

'Yes, but they think I'm somewhere near Leeds and happily married. The postmark would show I'm not.'

'Just think about it. That's all I'm saying. They are getting older and have no one else but you. That must be hard for them, even though you've obviously not got on well. They deserve some consideration, don't you think?'

Jenny walked off and couldn't help wondering how Beth had found herself so far South in a mental hospital and now here in Dover, just so far from home. Meanwhile Beth considered miserably what Jenny had just said and knew deep down she was right. She couldn't blank out her past for ever.

CHAPTER EIGHT

Dave had reached Folkestone and decided to stay the night there. He found a really cheap and run-down B&B which he could barely afford but at least he'd get a good breakfast to see him on his final way to Dover for the ferry and that elusive freedom he'd been searching for. For several nights he'd had a recurring nightmare of whizzing wheels spinning out of control and bodies and souls flying off lost into the universe. He had no idea what it all meant, but it made for disturbed nights and tired mornings. He was worried about money, but thought he'd get to France before looking for a job. He could brush up his French, which had been quite good at school, but which he'd hardly used since. His walk that day was bright and autumnal, and he really enjoyed the colours of gold and rust on the remaining leaves on the trees. He went cross-country and followed his instincts with the sun in roughly the right place to get him to Dover. He wasn't in a hurry. Foot passengers could always get on the ferries. He probably walked at least an extra five miles, but he reached Dover at sunset and went down to the docks. He bought his ticket and sat with a polystyrene cup of instant coffee while he waited the hour for the next ferry.

He decided to have a leg stretch and wandered outside looking up at the old castle. Coming down the steep road was a figure, a youngish girl swinging a shopping bag with her head bent down, so he didn't recognise Beth until she was almost parallel. His heart thumped. Was this part of a dream? A nightmare? Had she seen him? He turned his back and hurried inside just as she looked up. He couldn't see if she had seen him or not. He ran inside the terminal and queued to get on the next ferry, which had arrived. He knew he was such a coward, but what could he do? He didn't want the recriminations, the emotional turmoil, and the feelings of being trapped. He didn't want to know about the abortion. He simply didn't want to revisit that time and place at all. For a second time he abandoned Beth. And yes. She had seen him, and her heart too was thumping and banging in her chest. Her emotions were incredibly mixed. There in front of her was the man who had got her pregnant, whom she had loved with all her heart, who had deserted her and left her to cope on her own with a traumatic abortion which hadn't worked, then the pain of labour, then a baby she couldn't care for and the separation and adoption. Beth simply stared as she saw his retreating back. She was rooted to the spot, with fear, anger and misery running through her veins. She'd popped out to get a few bits for the supper and needed to get back and cook. Why, why had she chosen to come this long way out of her way? If she'd kept to the upper road, she would never have seen Dave. She'd never have had to face up to all this baggage from her past. She sat down shakily on a bench and tried to gather herself together. She had at least the presence of mind to phone the home and say she might be late doing the supper. Jenny answered the phone and said not to worry. She would warm up the stew Beth had made earlier and use the smash potato instead of the real ones Beth had gone out to buy.

'Are you OK?' asked Jenny

'No. Not really.' Answered Beth, 'but I will be in a little while'

'See you soon. Don't worry about anything. We'll find time to talk when you get back. Take care'

CHAPTER NINE

By Saturday morning Jade was hooked on Rosa, on the flat, on Lucca and on all things Italian. Never had she woken feeling so happy and fulfilled and blissful. Never had her relationships been anything more than physical lusts and infatuations. Now she felt she knew what it was to be in love.

She waited for each footfall of Rosa coming in and out, breathed in the scent of her skin and her clothes, and longed for the nights to start all over again.

Rosa was a student, studying business and doing art in her spare time. Jade spent the days out drawing and the evenings cooking for them both and creating clothes and bags out of scraps of material which she'd found in a market.

On Saturday morning at half past five she crawled out of their bed and started to pack up her paintings. She had decided to sell any or all of them. She wouldn't return to England and the cold, nor seek a place at Art College the next year. She would stay here with Rosa forever, and enjoy this amazing relationship with her other half, whom she had found so serendipitously.

Rosa likewise seemed smitten. They spent hours in the double bed together getting to know each other and continually feeling their emotions running away with them.

Jade sold three paintings on the first Saturday and, as they went for 100 euros each, she took home 270 euros and they went out on the town, bought a bottle of wine and went dancing. It was the first time they had been out together, and the first time Jade had any qualms about the way Rosa had 'picked her up' in the café.

Instead of wrapping herself round Jade all evening Rosa, flirted and danced with about six other people. Whether girls or boys they were subjected to her wide grin and magnetic charm. At the end of the evening Jade couldn't find Rosa. She walked round and round the café bar, trying to get through the throng of hot bodies. Several slightly drunk men groped her as she passed and feeling extremely churned up and anxious, she returned to the little flat. There was a light on, and she rushed up the steps, hoping Rosa hadn't been taken ill, which would explain her going off without saying goodbye. At the top of the stairs, she halted briefly and heard noises from within. Rosa was not alone. This was strange. Jade walked in boldly and to her humiliation and horror found Rosa in bed with a gorgeous thin Italian boy looking like an Adonis.

'Come in', said Rosa through a haze of smoke, which Jade reckoned was marijuana, 'let's have a threesome'

The world seemed to shake as Jade sat down suddenly on the floor. She was too overwhelmed even to cry. What a fool she had been thinking this was the love affair of her life. Yes. She had fallen hook, line and sinker for this beautiful Rosa, but her love was not reciprocated at all. Rosa was using her for self-gratification, just as Jade had used so many boys in the past.

Quietly she packed her small rucksack and her art things while Rosa continued to enjoy noisy sex in front of her with the new boy.

She stumbled out of the little flat without even saying goodbye and ran down the stairs and back up to the main square. At least she had enough money to get on a train or a bus and get away.

She went down to the bus station and got on an overnight bus. She didn't even stop to see where it was heading. It was going to Munich and would take nearly a day and a half. All through the long night she wept quietly, her heart broken and sore, her tears making her face blotchy and running down into her neck, making her collar wet. She abandoned herself to an absolute grief, such as she had never known. Her mind ran back over the last few months, her relationship with Dave, her decision to come abroad to paint, her application for Art College and now this abortive love affair, which made her realise how she had used men and how her heart was eventually won by a woman. She felt crushed and broken and eventually on the second leg of the journey fell into an exhausted sleep. On arrival at the bus station, she realised she hadn't a clue what to do.

The bus had arrived at 4a.m. and the streets were shining with the night's rain. Jade found a café and pointed to the coffee, holding out her money which was fortunately euros

'Thank goodness we at least have a shared currency,' she thought.

She needn't have worried. In a city like this everyone spoke English.

What on earth should she do next?

The last forty-eight hours had been a wakeup call. She felt isolated, bruised and battered by life. She remembered the kindness of the old lady who had let her sleep on her bed, and longed suddenly to be at home, to be in a stable place where she really belonged. She sat at the café on the edge of the bus station and sorted out her purse. There was quite a bit of her money left from the sale of the paintings. On the spur of the moment, she went to the ticket office. Would there be a bus to London later that day? Yes. She could get to Calais, cross by ferry and there would be a different bus at Dover to take her on to London. Poor Jade felt as if the trip to Italy had been the last she would ever do. There had been so much hope, anticipation and joy in her initial idea to get away from it all. She had been glad to leave behind the louche way of life she'd had for the last few years. She'd been intent on focussing her thoughts on becoming serious about her art and attempting to get qualified as an art teacher. Her drawings were good, she knew that, and people even wanted to buy her work. The only thing was that her relationships, particularly this thing with Rosa, messed with her head. She was world weary, tired of emotional upheaval and bodily exhausted from the travelling and odd eating.

The bus to Calais would take another eighteen hours. The train would be more expensive but take half that time. Jade decided she'd really had enough of these long-haul buses and took herself off to the station.

She managed to find a train and a seat and waited with a book in the waiting room, where she was surrounded by families with large numbers of squabbling and loud children. At least she had none of those to worry about. Eventually she picked up her small rucksack and her rolled up paintings and climbed wearily on to the train. Travel was becoming a burden not a joy.

CHAPTER TEN

Dave looked back as the ferry pulled out of the harbour. He could just about make out a small figure, hunched up on a bench in the area where he'd last seen Beth. Part of him was glad to have escaped, but mainly he felt rotten. He couldn't imagine having had such a narrow escape from meeting up with Beth after all these months. It must be more than a year since he'd seen her. What on earth was she doing in Dover anyway? He knew he'd behaved badly the first time round. This time it was even worse. He actually felt ashamed of himself. This was yet another feeling he wasn't used to and didn't like!

Try as he might to find something to do on the ferry or some people to talk to, he couldn't get his mind off the sight of that forlorn little figure all alone on a bench. It stuck in his head like a Lowry painting with a solitary body in it. Dave bought some food and settled down with the film, but he couldn't concentrate. The sooner he reached France, the better. If he were in a different country, he could perhaps distance himself from these feelings of self-loathing. He sat back on the hard seat and closed his eyes. Meanwhile unbeknown to him, his other recent attachment was winging her way across the continent towards the very port at which he was due to arrive. Jade's journey through Germany was going at considerable speed on the train, and despite the two rough days she'd had, she realised she was enjoying this ride. It really was worth the extra expense to be able to get up and walk down a corridor when you wanted, buy drinks or food, and see the countryside so much better. Her ticket was to Calais. She had decided not to go straight through to London. She had nowhere to go and if she caught the ferry across as a foot passenger it would give her time for reflection. She could save a bit too. The train eventually arrived at Calais and Jade got off, gathered her small belongings and made her way to the ferry. She really had had enough of travelling. The weariness of movement almost overcame her, but she pushed forward into the queue of backpackers and was soon on board the warm and cosy ferry. She found a seat and collapsed into it, hoping to sleep for the voyage. Alas, a family with a tired and grumpy three-year-old sat next to her and she was simply too exhausted to get past them to escape to another part of the boat. It was the end of half term, and the boat was heaving. She might not find another seat, so it was best to stay put by the window and put in her earplugs or listen to her iPlayer. Even that seemed beyond her. The ferry moved out slowly into the channel and she was off, back towards England, English food and weather and a long winter ahead.

CHAPTER ELEVEN

Dave sat on the ferry to France and thought through his options. He had realised that finding Jade was going to be impossible. He had no forwarding address, and much as he fancied being with her again, he knew there were other women around. They weren't all needy, like Beth, and many of them would play around with him quite happily without seeking commitment. He was so tired of this running away. Perhaps finding a wife wasn't such a bad idea. He simply didn't see how he could settle anywhere yet. When he reached France, he would stay in one place, maybe for three months, and find a job. Things were so much easier now they let you work in the EU without restrictions. He didn't fancy the cold of Northern France. It would be no better than England, but maybe he could hitch a lift with a lorry going to Marseilles or somewhere like that. He made his way to the place where the lorry drivers went for their meals, and talked his way in. Once settled at a table he was able to charm his way into finding out which drivers were going south, and to use his natural charisma to get himself fixed up with a ride for the two-day drive. That being done he retired to his seat, which thankfully still had his jersey on it, and fell into a deep sleep. The crossing was quite rough, but nothing woke Dave and even his conscience seemed less bothersome.

On the other side of the channel all was not well. Jade started to feel incredibly seasick after half an hour and found her way to the nearest Ladies loo. She stayed there for most of the rest of the journey and could hardly get herself off the boat when it finally arrived in Dover. She felt wobbly and weak and her long days of travel plus the shock and the heartbreak she had suffered began to take their toll. She simply had to find somewhere for the night and the first place she saw at the top of the long hill which wound its way up away from the docks was the Salvation Army hostel. She knocked on the door and asked if they could take her in for the night. The warden took one look at her and rushed her upstairs to a very small box room where she could be on her own. She wasn't sure if the girl were just tired or maybe infectious with some disease. She wasn't taking any risks. Jade slept for nearly three days. Occasionally some quiet person would tiptoe into her room, top up her jug of water or bring her something to eat. They were so kind here, particularly that softly spoken girl who came and looked after her. On the third day she woke to find the girl gazing down at her with a breakfast tray in her hand.

'Are you feeling better this morning?'

'Goodness me. How long have I been here?'

'Three days and this is the first time you've really looked at me or been strong enough to speak.'

'I am so grateful,' said Jade, 'I don't know what I'd have done without your ministrations. Have you got time to sit with me while I eat this?'

'Not really,' said Beth, 'but I could come back a little later. I have to do the breakfasts, change the beds when there's a turnover, plan the evening meal and shop for it and then do the cooking'

'That's a lot to do' said Jade, 'I hope they pay you well?'

'O no,' replied Beth, 'I get my board and lodging for free in exchange for the work.'

'Really? That sounds extraordinary. Anyway, it would be lovely to have a bit of company when you've got the time. I've not had a proper conversation in weeks.'

Each girl left the other thinking there must be a story behind this and little knowing that they were already entangled in that strange way by having had a relationship with Dave.

When Beth returned, she found Jade holding a folded letter.

'Hi there. Come in. I have something I'd like to discuss with you.'

'Really?' said Beth, who had taken a liking to Jade, although she hardly knew her.

'Yes. I need to find a job. I want to apply for Art College next year and I need money and a place to live till then. I don't really mind where I go and looking through this copy of 'The Lady' my eye fell upon this ad. There's a house, up near Liverpool, but in the country. They are looking for a living-in couple to help with cooking, childcare and gardening. I love gardening and you obviously love cooking and I like kids too. Do you?'

Beth reeled at the thought of the child she had recently given up.

She had wanted it so badly but had landed up with a nervous breakdown and this awful emptiness. Could she take up a job looking after someone else's children? Well, why not. She needed to move on and here was someone asking her to go with them. Perhaps this was what she'd been waiting for.

'Didn't they mean a husband-and-wife team?'

'I don't know, but I could ring and ask. There's a phone number here at the bottom of the ad. Look, why don't you come back later, when you've had time to think about it and I'll get some more details. OK?'

CHAPTER TWELVE

The following morning Beth's mind was made up. It was a strange thought that she might be moving near to the area where she had told her parents she was living and happily married. It was three years since she had contacted them and after the last year and the traumas she had endured she realised that their bossy, interfering and superior manner towards her might be something other than what she had always thought.

As a teenager she had found their restrictions irksome. That summer when they had said she either did what they wanted or needn't bother getting in touch ever again, she had taken them at their word. There was just the one letter, to get them off her back, where she'd said she would be moving North, probably to the Wirral, she wasn't sure yet, and that her husband had a job which meant they would probably stay North. She realised now how hurtful it would have been for them not to have been invited to her wedding, which of course had never occurred. As for her three years of silence, she looked upon that now as unforgivable. Since she'd lost her baby, she realised what enormous attachment you felt for your own child, even when you couldn't cope with it emotionally.

Her mother had been quite unsuitable to become a mother. Nevertheless, she had been given a home with two parents; she'd had food, clothes and schooling and plenty of discipline, if not hugs and affection. Her parents had cared for her in their own way, and she had returned their love, such as it was, with indifference and hostility. If only she hadn't lied to them about getting married. Beth roamed around the big Salvation Army Hostel looking at the rooms where she had worked happily now for many weeks. She had arrived at the end of the summer, and it was now October, not the best time of year to be moving North at all, but how often would an opportunity arise for a paid position in a house with free accommodation thrown in and a car as well. She also realised that she would be moving back nearer the Peak District and her parents. Also, alas, nearer to Manchester where she had first met Dave.

She went and knocked on Jade's door.

'Hi. Can I come in?'

'Yes of course,' said Jade grinning from her bed, 'well is it yes, or no?'

'Definitely yes, if they'll have us both.'

'O, Brilliant. I spoke to the housekeeper this morning. They are desperate to fill the posts straight away. The couple who were there were Polish and left with no notice saying there was illness back home. As long as we can help with children, gardening and cooking they don't mind if we're not a husband-and-wife team. They probably think we're a couple of dykes, but never mind.'

Beth blanched at the very idea, but Jade laughed it off and said, 'Have you told them here yet that you might be leaving?'

'No. I wanted to talk to you first, but I'm off downstairs now and I'll talk to Jenny as soon as I see her'

Beth went down feeling excited and scared. When she told Jenny there was the possibility of a semi-permanent live-in job and that she and Jade were going to apply together she was greeted with a huge hug and,

'I am so glad for you. I knew you would have to move on from here. We do love your cooking, but we can't employ people here on a permanent basis. We simply don't have the funding. Did you make up your mind about trying to find out who adopted your baby and see whether you could get her back?'

Beth sighed deeply and looking Jenny in the eye replied,

'I've thought about nothing else for weeks. I realise it would be thoroughly selfish of me to tear her away from people who have loved her since she was born, and I also realise I'm not ready for that sort of commitment on my own. I'd have to leave her with someone else all day in order to work and it would be no life for a child at all. I am so glad to have been here with you lot. I've found calmness and a new perspective on life I never knew before. I might even become a Christian one day.'

Jenny hugged her and Beth realised she was actually crying.

Beth's last words before hurrying on to do breakfasts were

'Are you willing to write me a reference?'

'Of course,' said Jenny, 'and a testimonial too.'

Beth returned to Jade's room and Jade said she would phone the house and tell them her friend would like to apply too. It was so easy now. They could send their CV's and references by email and attach photos of themselves and a letter of application.

Mrs. Murphy, who was the housekeeper given the job of finding help, was delighted by their quick response. She told Jade that the household was pretty chaotic without the cooking and childcare. The gardening could wait as it was October, but really, she wasn't managing on her own. She even said that if she could speak to the Director of the hostel, she might accept their application there and then.

Later that day all was organised. It would be a three-month contract only, just so Beth and Jade could see how they liked it up there and so Lady Mawes could be satisfied with their work. There was the problem of lack of experience with small children. There were two, a boy of nearly one and a little girl of three, but Lady Mawes was young and energetic and a full-time mother. What she needed was a spare pair of hands around and a permanent babysitter living in, so she could continue her social lifestyle.

They sent a photo of the house and gardens down to Beth and Jade and they gasped in awe. The house looked incredibly old and huge. It was called Ambersleigh Hall and was in the countryside outside Liverpool. It looked quite remote, and it was obvious from the photos that the driveway was overgrown and that the creepers on the house needed pruning. Beth thought it looked slightly scary, but Jade couldn't wait to get up there and start drawing. Jenny told them that the Sally Army had a fund for extraordinary circumstances and sent both girls out into the town.

'Go and buy yourselves some thermal underwear and a warm jacket of some sort. It will be much colder up there, and that house looks freezing. I expect it is horribly damp but isn't this exciting? - a new start for you both.'

CHAPTER THIRTEEN

Dave followed the loudspeaker instructions when they arrived in Calais, but instead of making his way to the door allocated for foot passengers he made his way on to the lorry deck and found his driver. He had a passport, so it didn't really matter that he had boarded as a foot passenger and left in a vehicle. The cab was so high up it took three large steps to get up into it and the comfortable seating and the driver's sleeping arrangements amazed Dave. The driver was friendly but fairly taciturn. He didn't mind having a passenger, but he concentrated hard and left Dave to his own thoughts. The miles were quickly passing and when the driver had to stop for his essential breaks Dave was happy to wander off and inspect the village or town where they had landed up. He tried his French out in various places and was happy to find it less rusty than he thought. After a solid day of driving, plus the regular breaks, they landed up in Pau, which was far further West than Dave had hoped. His lorry driver took him to a transport café and introduced him to some mates. He was lucky enough to find someone going to Marseilles and thought he'd get there and then try to move on to Cannes. It was so good not to be in the wet and cold of England, even though the French

Autumn was quite advanced. Dave put his mind to what work he could do. He hoped to get something using his computer skills and felt that a small firm might be better than a bigger outfit. He spent a night in Marseilles and realised that he would have to get work soon or go hungry. He had barely enough for the one-star hotel which turned out to be a sort of youth hostel with two double bunks in each room and a shared bathroom along the corridor. They offered a typical continental breakfast of baguette and jam with a large bowl of thin milky coffee. At least that would get him going for the day. At eight o'clock he was on the streets looking around and marvelling at how big a place this was. He had replaced his stolen rucksack with one he'd found on a skip, but all the straps were broken, and he'd done a Heath Robinson effort with string. That couldn't last long either. Eventually he found himself in some sort of square and sat down on a wall. There were quite a few young men hanging around there, looking as if they were waiting for something and when a bus turned up he asked where they were all off to. 'They are hiring casual workers today on the new building site. Apparently, there's been a 'flu' bug and lots of the builders are off work and the company is behind on its building schedule. If you're looking for employment hop on the bus with us. I'm sure they'll use you too. Its unskilled work, carrying the bricks to the brickies and wheeling barrows around. You look dirty enough anyway' said the French boy laughing as he shoved his way into the bus queue. 'Oh well. Beggars can't be choosers,' Dave thought and pushed his way with the other lads on to the heaving bus. It struck him there must be a lot of unemployment if there were so many people after this one day's work.

He got off with the others at the building site and realised he was by no means the only foreigner: many of them looked like illegal immigrants, Roma or African.

Dave got his name on the list and was given a hard hat. This was all a bit different from sitting at a desk, being a student, or swanning around England on foot, walking miles and getting fit. Never had he done such a hard day's work in his life. By the end of it his back and leg muscles were shouting at him. He had nowhere to go to sleep and the pay was a few measly euros. He felt angry and exploited, but nevertheless agreed to return the next day. He had to have some sort of work, and this was better than nothing. It turned out there was a hostel for the workers from abroad which would cost only 10 euros, so he trudged off with the others, occasionally trying to converse in a mixture of halting French and pidgin English. What a time to come to France, approaching winter, without sufficient clothing and hoping to find some cushy employment. He must have been mad. The hostel was very basic and smelt of drains and garlic. The bunks were narrow and metallic grating was heard every time someone turned over. Dave slept fitfully, anxious about catching fleas or something worse. The pay at the end of that day gave him enough for a bus fare to Cannes or a slap-up meal. He chose neither. He started walking along the coast road and managed to thumb a lift from a lorry. The driver was Bulgarian and spoke no French and little English, but enough to nod his head when Dave said

'Cannes?'

At least now he was on his way to his chosen destination.

CHAPTER FOURTEEN

Jade and Beth took their meagre belongings on to the train and were waved off by a sad but friendly Jenny. She had enabled them to get a train instead of a bus and arranged for them to have at least enough money to get them to Liverpool and buy themselves a lunch. She was pleased to see two such friendly and feisty youngsters beginning to get on with their lives. She had so many sad cases of inadequate people who became dependent on the sort of help the Salvation Army could give. These two were a success story and she wished them well.

Beth offered to go and fetch a cup of tea from the buffet and when she returned Jade had put their bags in the overhead rack, leaving out the letters from Ambersleigh Hall with the maps and information. There was a book about the history of the place, which Lady Mawes had sent and which they'd not had time to read. The whole question of money had been left in the air. They knew very little about anything and this journey was to be their concentrated time together to get sorted. They sat side by side with the high backs of the seats in front and behind them forming a sort of cocoon. There was so much to think about and plan. Jade looked first at the history and kept interrupting Beth with

'Wow' and 'No way!' and 'Just listen to this!'

It turned out the house went back to Jacobean times and that the Mawes family had lived there for generations. They had been Royalists and farmers but kept away as much as they could from wars. They had kept beef cattle and bees, for donkeys' years, and were a successful family, having produced loads of sons, heirs and spares. The current Lord Mawes sat in the House of Lords and had retained his hereditary title and seat. Lady Mawes had been a society girl from a wealthy banking family. She was only twenty-six and had these two gorgeous children. Her husband was forty-two and rather serious, but the gossip said they adored each other.

'Have you ever been near a house like this before?' asked Jade.

'Never. Well, I did once visit a National Trust property with my parents.'

'Do you know that's the first time you've ever mentioned your parents to me. Are they still alive? Do you see them much?'

Beth blushed and realised that talking to Jenny at the Sally Army hostel was one thing but opening up to this new friend quite another. It was habitual with her to lie her way out of uncomfortable situations but being in Dover for the last few weeks had made her think a lot about many aspects of her life. Should she tell Jade the truth? If she did, she risked her new friend despising her. If she lied, she would have to go on living that lie and she realised what deep water that got her into.

'Actually, I haven't spoken to them for three years. We fell out and

I just left home. They think I'm happily married and living in the North somewhere.'

Jade laughed.

'Well, you are nearly in the North, but not happily married. We're not even lovers.'

At this Beth blushed again. Something in her wanted to tell Jade more about this last year. She felt her past hung between them like a heavy curtain.

'How about you? Do you have a family somewhere?'

Jade laughed again.

'O yes. Dozens of them. I have a dad in London, a mum in Birmingham, a brother in Australia, a sister in Walsall and another in Ireland. I'm the youngest and we're all arty. I suppose that's why I want to go to Art College. My parents both went, and dad is a lecturer now at Birmingham Art College. He's a graphics designer and mum teaches photography. They split up when I was three, so I've been shoved around between them for years with different partners they've each had, but thank goodness, no half-brothers or sisters to add to the complication.'

'I wish I'd had at least one sibling,' said Beth.' It makes me angry that being the only one causes me to feel guilty at abandoning my parents, but they actually said they never wanted to see me again if I wouldn't comply with their wishes.'

'What was it they were asking of you that was so awful?'

Beth thought back to that conversation and realised it had been something entirely trivial. It wasn't that they had asked the impossible, it was the fact that at the age of twenty they had felt they could still tell her what to do and how to behave.

She realised that flouncing out of the house had been a childish response and the bitterness of her feelings somewhat unjustified. What a mess her life had turned into since.

She sighed deeply and Jade put an arm around her shoulder.

'Listen, why don't you get in touch. Send them a letter if they're not on email and tell them you're really sorry and would like to see them again. They must be desperate to know where you are and whether you're OK'

Beth swallowed and said,

'I'll think about it'

They were nearing their destination and their excitement was growing.

CHAPTER FIFTEEN

Dave climbed down from his last cab ride and looked about him. The driver had dropped him off on the hills looking down over the huge sweep of the 'golfe de la Napoule' bay. It was magnificent and Dave had thoughts of the film festival, the glamorous stars, the red carpet and the fantastic lifestyle of the wealthy in these parts. He knew he had a long way to go as he looked down at his dirty shoes, his shabby clothes and his meagre belongings. At least he was in the South of France, but where should he start in his rags to riches ambition?

He headed off down the hill towards the glittering sea. Even though winter was coming on it felt mild in comparison with the English climate he had just left. It was really quite delightful to be able to sling his coat over his shoulder as he walked. With not a care in the world Dave sped up his walking and worked his way down through the town. He walked for over an hour, stopping finally at the waterfront and looking about him.

He found a café/bar and ordered a coffee. When it came, he picked up an abandoned paper and started to look through the job ads.

'Vous desirez la travaille, uh? Je peux pouvoir vous aider'

'Mais oui,' said Dave looking up at the proprietor of the café.

He was a little Frenchman with a typical small moustache and the classical outfit of black with a white pinnie. This really seemed to be Dave's lucky day.

Here was a café right on the waterfront and he was being offered a job.

'I need a boy at the back to do the washing up and make the coffee pots ready. I don't pay much but there is an attic room you can have if you're prepared to keep an eye on the café at nights and investigate any disturbances.'

Washing up! Well maybe he'd start there and work his way up into a more responsible position. It had the advantage of coming with accommodation and of being within a stone's throw of the beach.

Next day Dave didn't know what had hit him. The proprietor wanted him to start cleaning the kitchen at 6a.m. and serve coffees from 6.30. The café was heaving with men on their way to work. They spoke a very fast patois which he couldn't keep up with and he found himself running around clearing, washing, drying and serving. There was no dishwasher. He was it. The bed had been lumpy and narrow. The bedding slightly musty and damp smelling and yet he was here, and he had a job and he was needed. What should he do? The line of least resistance beckoned as usual and after three days Dave felt almost that he belonged here. He was enjoying the winter sunshine, sand between his toes, French food and lots of cheap wine.

CHAPTER SIXTEEN

Beth and Jade had finally arrived and were awestruck with the sight of the building which up until then they had seen only in photos.

It nestled down in a valley with hills rising on three sides of it and the remains of some wonderfully laid out gardens in the front with views down to a river. It was stunningly beautiful and reminded the girls of costume dramas they had seen. It turned out that the family had hired it out to several TV and film companies to use as a set. They were pretty desperate for enough money to keep running the place, and this was a good way to do it. On closer inspection it was obvious that the paint was peeling off the outside walls and inside it was worse. There were damp patches in rooms on the East side where driving rain had entered through places where the guttering had gone. Over the next few days Beth and Jake explored and found damp smelling rooms, not in use, with old floral wallpapers peeling off the walls. None of this mattered. Lady Mawes was friendly if a little distrait. She had come from a wealthy family where there had been nannies and cleaners and lots of help. Much as she loved her husband, home and children, it was becoming ever more difficult to keep up the running of this huge house when they could afford to employ so few people. She wasn't in the least snobbish, but neither had she expected to do quite so much hands-on housework herself. When she met Jade and Beth, she almost cried.

'I am SO glad there are two of you. My husband is away such a lot and there is no one else living in. The housekeeper who hired you on our behalf lives in that little cottage you passed on the drive. It gets really lonely being here on my own at night. We have the dogs of course but they're not as good company as humans! Come on up and I'll show you your rooms. I wonder if you'd mind making up your own beds. I've put out the linen, but I simply haven't found time to do it today, my cleaner doesn't come in on a Saturday, and Mrs. Murphy has been looking after the children as I had to go to a charity function.'

Beth and Jade followed her up the wide wooden staircase on to a half-landing where Lady Mawes turned left. There were about six rooms along here and she asked if they would be happy to sleep near the children's nursery and listen out for them at night. She herself had the room at the end of the corridor and the children shared a huge room next to hers with an adjoining door.

Jade and Beth would have two rooms on the opposite side of the corridor. They looked out over an enclosed quadrangle at the back of the house, but they were warm, being above the kitchens where an aga was always lit. The girls were enraptured and speechless with delight. They had expected to be put in the attic like 'Upstairs, Downstairs'

Lady Mawes smiled at their excitement. I might just ask you to move if I have guests to stay. This is really the only part of the house we can afford to keep warm, so most of the time we'd rather have everybody closer together. If you go exploring the house with the children, you can go anywhere you want, but please put tights on Alice and extra jerseys on all of you. I must warn you the house is mainly cold and damp and there will be days up here when the weather is so awful you won't be able to get out in the grounds to exercise the little ones, and you will need to use up their abundant energy inside.'

She smiled at them.

'When you've made your beds, unpacked and settled in, just find your way back to the kitchen and we'll have some tea.'

The children were delightful, polite but full of fun.

'I'm Alice,' said the little girl, 'and that's Charles, He can't talk yet, but I always know what he wants so just ask me.'

CHAPTER SEVENTEEN

Jade and Beth, like Dave in France, settled down to new routines. The children woke early and wanted to come down, in their dressing gowns, at about six o'clock for warm milk. They were full of energy and the older girls found they had their work cut out to occupy them when it was too cold or wet to go out of doors. They were glad to explore the different rooms and to find old toys in an attic nursery. One of these had been a magnificent rocking horse and Jade set to work to restore it to its former glory. Alice helped to rub it down and then they painted it white with black splodges on the sides. Beth made it a new mane which they glued on with superglue and even Charlie watched entranced as Alice rode on it rhythmically and magically distant with a faraway look in her eyes. On fine days they walked long distances, with Charlie gurgling in an old pram with high wheels and an amazing leather interior. Lady Mawes said it had been in the family for years and she believed she herself used to be put outside to sleep in it. Alice had learnt to use a scooter, but often Beth or Jade would carry this while Alice ran around, picking flowers, climbing over dead branches or simply running in circles. She was a child with a huge imagination and easy to entertain.

Beth would slip away and plan and cook meals for them all, and as they settled in Lady Mawes began to relax and look less tired. 'How on earth I managed without you two, I can't imagine,' she said one day 'You will stay permanently won't you?'

Jade replied that she was still intending to go to art college the following September but wondered whether she might apply to Edinburgh and still keep in touch from there.

Beth replied that she had no other plans and would be delighted to stay on indefinitely.

It was still in Beth's mind that she ought to contact her parents and tell them where she was and what she was doing.

Having unburdened herself to Jade, she found it easier to talk about things. They spoke of their parents and childhoods, but still never mentioned any relationships they had had. It was a private world of each, which they were unwilling to share. Beth realised how far she had come from the broken girl in the mental hospital. She really didn't want anyone knowing about that episode.

Jade thought how far she had come since her trauma in Lucca and the broken heart she had returned with from Italy. During her illness at the Salvation Army hostel in Dover, she realised how juvenile she had been, and how real love was not the lust and passion she had previously found so exciting.

As the days grew shorter and they spent more time together she realised how fond she had become of Beth and that this real deep friendship was of more importance to her than the physical and emotional passions of the last few years. Her paintings began to show a state of peace and beauty in them as she drew the old house with its fading splendour and damp ivy clad walls.

She tried her hand at portraiture, especially the children when they were asleep, and eventually Lady Mawes said they would put on an exhibition of her work in the summer to help raise funds for her degree.

The days drew on towards Christmas and Beth knew that the time had come to contact her parents, however difficult that would be. One day she just sat down in the kitchen, and while the supper was cooking, she put pen to paper.

It was a simple message of regret and apology for her behaviour. She told them she had taken a long time to come to her senses and grow up. She told them that she hoped for reconciliation and gave her the address where she was living. She did not tell them about the lies, the false claim of marriage nor about the abortion, but she did say she was working at the big house as a nanny and cook. She posted it and waited.

CHAPTER EIGHTEEN

On Christmas Day Dave sat in his damp little attic room and contemplated his past and his future. He cast his mind back over so many childhood Christmases with a stocking on the end of his bed, a fire lit in the living room, warmth, comfort and family love. He heard the church bells ringing and decided that his French was certainly good enough now for him to follow a service. He phoned his parents and wished them a happy Christmas and could hear his mother sniffing at the other end if the phone,

'When are you coming home dear?'

'Soon,' he replied, 'very soon.'

And he realised he meant it. He had had enough of travelling, excitement, escape and foreign living. As he dressed in his shabby and none too clean clothes, he also realised that he was thinner and poorer than he had ever been. His dreams of wealth and success had come to very little, and he felt a failure. He wandered down to the church where people were dressed in their Sunday best, and where everyone else seemed to know each other. Lonely and somewhat depressed he sat near the back and wished they were singing the favourite Christmas carols he knew so well. After the service, where no-one had spoken to him, he returned to his flat, packed his small bag, wrote a note of apology to the café owner and locked himself out for the last time, dropping the keys back through the letter box. What a Christmas to remember.

Meanwhile Beth and Jade had dressed their little charges in their best clothes and dolled themselves up too. Lord and Lady Mawes, Mrs. Murphy the housekeeper, and Alice and Charlie walked the half mile to the Church on the estate. It was a crisp December day, with clouds scudding over the hills and a cold wind. Alice was allowed to take her scooter and Charlie had a pushchair which he chose to push rather than sit in. They laughed and joked as they walked along, and Beth felt she had never been happier. She had heard nothing from her parents and that saddened her. It had been three weeks since she wrote, but then they might have been away and not yet received her letter. Her imagination ran to all sorts of things. Maybe their love had turned to anger and hatred, because she had left them alone so long. Maybe one of them had died and she didn't even know.

The local congregation had turned out in full for the Christmas morning service and Jade and Beth felt very important being ushered to the front pews with their employers. The singing of the Christmas hymns and carols lifted the spirits of all. Even little Alice sang 'Away in a manger' with the Sunday school children, to the immense pride of her loving parents.

The walk back was jolly too, but as they neared the house Mrs. Murphy said to Jade and Beth, 'I shall need you in the kitchen for the next hour or so. There is so much to do and quite a lot of visitors coming for the big traditional lunch.'

'Fine,' said the girls, 'but don't you need one of us to help with the children?'

'No thanks,' replied Lady Mawes, ' this is really family time and we are going to do the presents upstairs.'

'Never mind,' said Jade, putting a consoling arm around Beth, 'we'll have our own presents later. After all we are being paid to work here'

'Yes. Of course,' replied Beth with a sigh as she thought of those lovely children upstairs while they slaved away over the lunch. She knew they didn't really belong and would never be part of the family, but she experienced that sadness of feeling like an outsider. Jade was already thinking ahead to Art College, but Beth felt it deeply. This place had become like home to her, and she wished more than anything that she had a real home of her own. They worked hard, cooking and preparing the big feast and at half past one all was ready. They had heard the imposing front doorbell ring several times, but each time Mrs. Murphy had leapt up and said,

'I'll go' so Jade and Beth had stayed in the kitchen. Finally, a bell sounded from the dining room and Mrs. Murphy said to the girls, 'You go on up and when His Lordship is ready, he'll ask you to come down and help to carry the food in'

Jade raced ahead and Beth followed. They entered a heaving drawing room, full of smart county people, but Lady Mawes welcomed them like long lost friends and said to Beth,

'There's a couple over there by the window that I'd particularly like you to meet.'

She led the way round the corner of the L shaped room and there, standing by the window were Beth's mum and dad.

First there was shock, then tears, then long hugs and kisses and squeezes and joy.

'O my darling, darling girl - we thought we might never see you again. As soon as we received your letter, we rang the house here and spoke to the housekeeper. She handed us over to Lady Mawes and we hatched this little plot. She has found it so hard not to tell you, but we wanted to surprise you and I think we were half afraid you might run away again if you knew we were coming.'

Lady Mawes insisted that Beth stay with her parents, and she found some of the visiting youngsters to go and help Jade bring in the lunch. Alice and Charlie were sitting adoring their father, one each side. He was very special because he had to spend such a lot of time away in London, so when he was home, they hung on to him, and barely looked at anyone else. It was the happiest Christmas day ever.

CHAPTER NINETEEN

Dave reached the main road at about 10 o'clock and realised that travelling on Christmas Day was a stupid mistake. No one was going anywhere. They were all at home enjoying a day off with their families. He wouldn't be able to hitch a lift and as ever he was strapped for cash.

The weather was bright and crisp. He started to walk and was glad he had at least brought a map. He wished his shoes were stronger if he was going to have to walk all day. He counted his money and knew he had to keep enough for food and shelter, which meant hitching or walking all the way back to Calais.

There were no buses anyway and no Lorries either. By lunchtime he was ravenous. He had brought no food with him and although he could quench his thirst in the streams, he wished he had a bar of chocolate, or indeed anything at all to eat. He felt like a character out of Dickens. Was it Oliver or David Copperfield who had walked all day without food? He couldn't remember. He realised his mind wasn't as sharp as it used to be and began to have self-doubts about his ability to get a job back in the UK in computing. His arrogance was gone. His confidence was gone, and a new self-awareness and knowledge replaced it. Perhaps, after all, this was what travelling and gap years were all about?

His route kept mainly to main roads, just in case anyone should pass him, but no one did. At one junction he found an old cottage and knocked on the door. A growling and then loud barking greeted his knock, but no one came, so he trudged on again. At about teatime he found a village, sleeping like all the rest of France it seemed. One house had a car parked outside, so he knocked tentatively and a woman, somewhat inebriated, came to the door.

'Joyeux Noel, Madame,' Dave said in his best French, 'Avez vous un peu de nouriture pour moi? J'ai marche toute la jour et j'ai faim.'

'Hang on love. I don't speak the Lingo.'

'I don't either really,' laughed Dave, 'I'm sorry to bother you, but I'm absolutely starving. There isn't a single shop or café open, and I've walked from Cannes.'

'My gawd! On Christmas Day? You must be mad. Come on in and join the party. We're staying with some friends we met on holiday. I'm sure they won't mind.'

Dave was immensely grateful to sit down and be given food to eat. There were about eight people, very noisy and full of Christmas cheer. Dave sat quietly eating at the kitchen table, but when he made to go off again the husband of the woman who had opened the door asked him where he was off to.

'I'm on my way back to England. I shall just walk slowly and hope eventually for a lift.'

'Listen mate. We're off back to England tomorrow morning. We've got a car and we're happy to take you. Maybe you might chip in a bit for petrol.'

'Wow,' said Dave, 'It's as if all my Christmases have come at once!' and he laughed. They made arrangements for him to kip down on a sofa for the night and on Boxing Day he took up a small space on the back seat of the car between mounds of parcels and presents and unidentifiable packages. His luck had surely turned.

CHAPTER TWENTY

Beth's parents couldn't believe how lovely the Mawes family were. They felt somewhat overawed by the huge house and posh manners of these landed gentry, but they soon realised that there wasn't much money around, and that Lord Mawes had to work incredibly hard to make ends meet, with the constant demands on his finances running such a large estate. They were delighted to see that Beth was so at home here and in her element, looking after the little children and doing the cooking. It was obvious that she was valued and loved and had found herself a niche with wonderful people. They even found themselves being included in the chatter over Christmas lunch and despite the expensive clothes and county accents, they realised that all these county folk were just human beings like them, with families and friends, hurts, disappointments and anxieties. They began to relax and enjoy this extraordinary Christmas. Even Jade, whom they had disliked at first, seemed to have become a good friend to their daughter and although she was louder and more flamboyant, they saw that Beth was being brought out of herself by this more extrovert friend.

As evening approached, Beth's parents said their goodbyes and made sure that Beth was going to keep in touch regularly now. During the lunch she had taken courage and explained that she wasn't married and never had been. She apologised for the lies and the neglect, but her parents said they felt they had been at fault trying to organise her life so rigidly. They were just so happy to have her back there was no room for resentment or recriminations.

Jade had decided against ringing all her family, but as the evening wore on, she thought of her dad in London and her mum in Birmingham and thought she would ring one of them. Which one? She plumped for dad, but there was no answer, so when she phoned her mum's number, she was amazed to hear her dad's voice at the other end?

'Hi dad. It's me, Jade'

'Jade? Where the hell are you? We haven't heard from you for weeks. We hoped you'd come home for Christmas so we could tell you the news, but we hadn't got your new mobile number.'

'Well, you'll have it now, dad, but tell me what the news is. It sounds exciting.'

'Well. Your mum and I have decided to give it another go. Your sister is here with us, and Anthony in Australia has rung so we've told him and your phone call is the icing on the cake. Hey, Jackie, come here. Listen to who's on the phone. Here you are Jade. I'll pass you over to mum.'

There was a slight pause and then Jade's mum's voice, full of laughter and fun telling her how happy she was and how everything was working out so well and wishing Jade a happy Christmas and asking her when she was coming home and what she was doing and where she was, until Jade felt quite giddy with emotion, surprise, delight and exhaustion.

'Hi mum. I'm so glad about you and dad. I've got a fantastic job near Liverpool, but I'm due some time off. I'll ask if I can take next week and come home. Is that OK?'

'Brilliant,' said her mum, 'I can't wait to see you.'

CHAPTER TWENTY-ONE

The hairs rising on the back of his neck, Dave clung silently to the door handle of the old Ford and prayed silently that the man would either slow down or at least stop jabbering to his wife and waving both arms in the air at the same time. He must have seen Dave's face in the driving mirror because he roared with laughter, said 'when in France drive like the French eh?' and had gone even faster.

The journey was unpleasant in more ways than one. Mrs. insisted on eating or smoking or both, which made Dave feel rather sick in the back. He could hardly complain since he was getting a ride almost all the way home, but on the other hand his last £50 had gone into the petrol kitty. Mr. had leapt on him when he opened his wallet, grinned, seized the notes and said,

'that'll do. Thanks.' End of conversation. Dave wondered how such uncouth people had made friends with the French family but decided not to ask. He was so exhausted that he dropped off several times and that made the journey go faster. They stopped from time to time at service stations and realising they had in fact taken all his money he was bought a coffee and allowed to share in a snack. At Calais they drove into a huge warehouse-type hypermarket and large quantities of wines and spirits were bought and stowed in any gaps they could find. Dave's corner was diminished even further. He was heartily glad to see the back of those people on board, but they found him not far short of Dover and said they'd look out for him on the car deck. Since they had all his money, he agreed he'd like a lift as far as they were going. Rain and wind delayed their entry into the harbour and Dave was feeling queasy and exhausted as he climbed back into his narrow space. He was soon asleep again and only woke when his lift drew to a halt near Birmingham and turfed him out somewhat unceremoniously. He stood on the side of the squelchy road and looked about him. He hadn't intended to come to Birmingham at all. He knew no one there, and had no money for onward travel. When he tried to hitch a lift, he just got very wet, with drivers whizzing past him and going through puddles near him and driving off grinning. What a country. What a place. What on earth should he do? It was the day after Boxing Day. Somewhere along the line he had missed a day. He searched for his mobile phone and found it gone. Perhaps it had dropped out of his pocket on the back seat of that car? He couldn't ring his parents and had about an hour to go before dark. 'Hell's teeth', he said to himself as he trudged on down the road, half-heartedly sticking his thumb out from time to time.

Back at Ambersleigh Hall, Jade had arranged to take a few days off and Beth, who had now seen her parents, agreed to stay on at the hall on her own, and to take a break later after Jade returned.

The Maweses were happy for Jade to go and see her parents, so she packed a few clothes and set off. The car they had been lent had to be shared, but Beth was sure she wouldn't need it, so sent Jade off with her blessing, to see her newly-reunited parents. It was the day after Boxing Day and the roads were still quiet. Jade got into Birmingham at dusk and set her sights on getting home, but she needed to stop for petrol. The only open garage she could find was near the bypass and she pulled in and filled up. On the forecourt stood a very shabby and dejected figure, looking as if he'd had about enough of the day. Jade looked at him with sympathy. He'd not had a good Christmas by the look of him. As he realised he was being watched he looked up and their eyes met.

'O my goodness. It can't be,' said Jade

'It jolly well is,' said Dave 'Where the hell have you sprung from?'

'And you too, come to that'

'Hop in and I'll give you a lift. Where are you going?'

'I wish I knew,' said Dave.' I've been dropped off here because I hitched a lift and fell asleep. I thought they were taking me to London.'

'Where have you been for Christmas then?'

'Oh. On the road and in France.'

'Well come back with me and get yourself sorted. You look dreadful, but remember when we get inside, you're just a friend, a platonic friend. There's going to be no more riotous sex and no mention of our past to my parents.'

'Right you are,' said Dave and looked at her shortened hair. She wasn't the same anymore and neither was he. At present all he could think about was the possibility of a bath and a clean bed and maybe the opportunity to put his clothes in a washing machine. Darkness was falling when they arrived at Jade's home, and she had to explain the turn of events that had brought her back with a boy who was an old friend but not a boyfriend. Her parents were so pleased to have her home to celebrate their new togetherness that they hardly turned a hair and found a spare mattress for Dave to sleep on in the conservatory. He was offered a bath and the loan of some clean pyjamas and Jade's mum, taking pity on him, popped his clothes into the washing machine.

CHAPTER TWENTY-TWO

Beth found life without Jade rather dull. She had forgotten how much time she had on her hands in the evenings, once the children were in bed. Alice and Charlie were usually asleep by 6.30 or 7o'clock and she did the cooking during the day. The housekeeper was very sweet, but she lived out in the grounds and had little in common with Beth. Lady Mawes was often out at charity functions or dinner parties or else she was entertaining at home and Beth really wasn't part of all that. It gave her time to contemplate her position and her future. She realised that above all she wanted to settle down and be married herself and have children. It was all she had ever wanted, and she knew, although she had messed up with Dave, that it was right that their child was being given a good home and the love and care of two people who had really wanted her. Much as Beth fretted over the loss of her child, she knew that Dave had never really wanted a baby at all, had persuaded her to get rid of it and had disappeared off the map, when any commitment had been expected of him. Beth thought with sadness of how much she had loved him and how badly she had been let down. Despite all of that she felt she had never loved anyone that way before or since. Perhaps she never would.

Her mobile phone rang, and she was pleased to see Jade's number come up.

'Hi there. How are you? How are you managing without me? Do the kids miss me? What have you been up to?'

'Hang on,' said Beth 'Which of those questions would you like an answer to?'

They talked for ages until just before she rang off Jade mentioned she had met up with an old flame, who wasn't of any interest to her anymore, but who had cadged a few nights off her parents.

'He's really at a loose end and I wondered whether Lady Mawes might give him some work. There's so much to do around the place. The ivy needs cutting back. The house needs a lick of paint and Dave would be able to help with the computers and things like that too.'

'How strange,' said Beth,' I was just thinking about an ex of mine, also called Dave, who was into computers. Why don't you ring Lady Mawes and just ask her straight out if she can give some work to your friend?'

They rang off, still without any idea, after all these months that their Daves were one and the same person. Jade phoned her employers and asked if they wanted any extra help around the grounds or in the house. She mentioned that she had met up quite accidentally with an old friend who was a well-qualified computer expert but also pretty versatile. He could turn his hand to most things, and was currently at a loose end, having come back from travelling abroad for several months. He needed a job and some money. Lord and Lady Mawes said they couldn't afford any more help at present but would ask some of their friends. There the conversation ended

CHAPTER TWENTY-THREE

Dave woke with a sore neck, where he had bent it in his sleep trying to fit his long frame on the slightly short mattress on the floor. He got himself to the bathroom and realised as he surveyed the human wreck in the mirror that he was no longer the Adonis Jade had once hungered for. He thought what he most needed to do was shave and get a haircut. Returning to the conservatory he saw a neat pile of clean, if shabby, clothes sitting on the arm of a chair, neatly folded. At least he was now clean, and it wouldn't be long before he could tidy himself up a bit. He really needed to get a job, or borrow some money, and he was determined not to visit his parents until he had made something of himself. Youth and optimism were on his side, but the last few months had taken their toll on his confidence and his CV.

Jade was up and about and laughed when she saw him.

'I still can't believe in this coincidence of bumping into you at a service station after nearly a year. There is so much to catch up on. I have so much to tell you. I rang my employers last night after you fell asleep. They are going to ask around to see if anyone needs any sort of help. It probably will be manual work of some sort rather than computers, but it would be a start. I'll lend you enough to get a haircut at least and have a bit in your pocket.'

'Well, how have you been and where have you been. Did you get to Italy?'

'I sure did. I started a really good portfolio, and then I got side-tracked and sold a lot of my stuff and thought I'd stay in Italy, but it didn't work out. I've made a super new friend and we've got a job together in this fabulous old house near Liverpool. When I go off to Art College, I think Beth might stay there and become a proper nanny. She's a brilliant cook and loves children.'

'How strange', thought Dave, as yet again his thoughts came back to his old flame Beth and her desire for a child and her brilliant cooking. He sighed as he wondered what to make of his life, which seemed to be going nowhere. He thought the least he could do was tell his parents he was back in England, but before he made the phone call Jade came to him with the news that Lady Mawes had rung her to say some close friends of theirs would be delighted to have a computer expert come and sort out their business.

CHAPTER TWENTY-FOUR

The spring gradually unfolded. As the cool winds and showers swept across the Northern valleys, the Hall at Ambersleigh continued to be the damp, enchanting, much loved home of the Mawes family. It encompassed the extended menagerie of housekeeper, helpers, a spaniel puppy and visitors from friends of all the occupants. Beth's parents were always welcomed and even Jade's assorted family members were encouraged to visit. Lord and Lady Mawes were truly generous and friendly to all, but were hiding their financial problems behind a genteel façade of kindness and welcome. However, on one visit from Jade's father he bumped into Lady Mawes in the gardens.

'Good morning Mr. Prentice,' said Lady Mawes, in her usual friendly and welcoming fashion. 'Are you enjoying our gardens? They really need a little more work on them.'

'Do you mind if I say something?'

'Of course not,' replied Lady Mawes, 'Is it about Jade?'

'Well, I did want to thank you for all you have done for her, and especially for encouraging her to keep up her painting and creating that wonderful portfolio. She tells me you have offered to put on a solo exhibition in the summer here. I can't help noticing how much work needs doing on the place, and I wonder whether I can help in any way. I realise this may be a 'touchy' subject, but it does need addressing before the Hall becomes uninhabitable in that East wing.'

'O dear,' said his hostess, 'I didn't realise things looked so bad to an outsider. We aren't in the position to do much about it at present. My husband is determined not to sell off the land which has been in his family for generations, and without doing that the income from this property is really unequal to the demands made upon it.'

She sighed and looked back up to the house. The South front was so pretty, and she could see the children's nursery curtains billowing out as the room was aired. She loved those ivy clad walls so dearly, but looking at the East wing, she noticed more slipped roof tiles, and she knew that the gardening, which Beth did with some 'help' from the children, was not nearly enough. There was just so much to do and not enough time, energy or money to do it. Secretly she had begun to think they might have to make the house over to the National Trust and just keep a small flat in their wonderful property in perpetuity. She sighed again.

'What help did you think you might come up with?' she smiled at him rather ruefully.

'Well. It would be a huge change for you all, but as you seem so gregarious, friendly and sociable, I think it might be worth considering. I work for Birmingham University, but I also have a link with Liverpool University, and I know they want to extend their Art and Design courses to integrate Architecture and Horticulture. They need a new site, and more accommodation. A building like yours would be ideal. The students could live in, get the feel of our old country houses, work on the grounds for their Horticultural training, work on the restoration of the fabric of the building etc etc.

I am the chairman of the project as I've been associated with the Art school ever since I graduated from there, as did my wife. I would love to put this to the Senate as a possibility, and if it went ahead, you and Lord Mawes would be able to name your terms. I imagine you would keep your part of the house private and intact. After all, from what I've observed you only really live in one part of the house anyway, and the girls are sleeping in that wing too. I'm sorry if this seems very forward of me, but I've been getting quite excited at the possibilities this would afford for all of us. I'm sure you would want to have time to think this over carefully with your husband, but there is an important meeting of Senate in three weeks' time, and I could put this on the agenda, if there is any possibility of it happening.'

CHAPTER TWENTY-FIVE

Dave started his job the week after New Year. The friends of the Mawes family lived not that far away in Birkenhead. He kept in touch with Jade, being very grateful for her help in getting started again, but their relationship had become quite distant, and there was no intention on either side to pick up the short love affair they had enjoyed months ago.

Dave no longer thought about her, but every so often he thought about Beth. He wondered where she was, what she was doing and whether she had ever forgiven him for letting her down so badly. The more he thought about her sweet nature and trusting manner, the more he realised what a treasure he had let go, because of his selfishness. He went home several times and saw how happy his parents were as they aged together, friends as well as lovers. They sometimes bickered and he could see that there were odd things about each other that caused mild irritation, but apart from that they worked together as a team, they were committed and purposeful and loving and kind and generous. Dave went clubbing occasionally and looked for a girl, but, every time he thought he'd found someone, he felt they couldn't match up to the girl he had lost. He no longer looked for sex alone.

He wanted love and companionship and friendship and shared ideals. In fact, he realised he wanted what his parents had and what he had secretly despised and rejected.

The summer was coming on and his work was finished in Birkenhead, but he felt drawn towards Liverpool and found himself a job there programming. He rented a flat near the dockside and began to make some friends.

Meanwhile Beth and Jade were continuing to enjoy their work at Ambersleigh Hall. Jade did more of the childcare and left the cooking and gardening to Beth. In the evenings Jade retired to her makeshift studio and worked on her portraits of the family and the house. She was developing quite a style of her own and knew that this portfolio should get her into Art College, but she wished she could stay at Ambersleigh as well.

Instead of continuing to think of Edinburgh she decided to apply to Liverpool. After all, both her parents had trained there, and it would mean she could stay around this area. She was within commuting distance of the college. Could she remain as a part time nanny and manage to be a full-time art student. Would the Mawes family be agreeable to this?

She decided to apply first and work out the logistics afterwards.

Beth was absolutely convinced that she never wanted to leave either Ambersleigh Hall or the Mawes family. They were such lovely people and she had become devoted to Alice and Charlie.

Lord and Lady Mawes had spent several wakeful nights mulling over Mr. Prentice's proposal and had concluded that they really no longer needed to keep this huge house to themselves. They asked Mr. Prentice to send someone from Liverpool to discuss the way the plan might work, and exactly how the building could be separated so they would keep their private side of the house. It would be a huge and heartrending change, but on the other hand, as Lady Mawes looked out at the overgrown parterre, she could imagine students working all over it to bring it back to its former glory.

She loved having a house full of people and wouldn't mind a permanent base in a much smaller house. The only thing she dreaded was an enormous car park, but Mr. Prentice had promised this could be quite a way from the house on the North side and screened by trees.

It all seemed very hopeful.

CHAPTER TWENTY-SIX

The time had nearly come for the promised exhibition. Jade's paintings were ready, and she now had a confirmed place at Liverpool. When she told her parents, they were delighted that their daughter would be following in their footsteps. She was undoubtedly extraordinarily talented. Having used the paintings of the Mawes children as well as of Ambersleigh Hall in her portfolio in order to gain admission to Liverpool, she realised if she could sell some of these it would help to finance her course. She set about getting the best ones framed and then had to decide on pricing. This was always the most difficult part of showing one's work. If you over-priced it no one would buy. If you under-priced it people thought it wasn't any good or amateurish. Jade decided to go with the sort of pricing the man in Italy had offered her, maybe one hundred pounds or even one hundred and fifty, but some of them she put at two hundred and fifty. These were her favourites, and she didn't really want to sell them. It felt like parting with a child. She put the family portraits up as NFS as she reckoned they were private, but much to her surprise Lord Mawes came and said,

'Please put 'sold' on those instead of not for sale.'

'I'm sorry, I don't quite understand,' said Jade, rather taken aback 'I am buying the portraits of my children for my wife as her birthday present. How much do you want for them?'

'O, I can't possibly charge you,' replied Jade, feeling rather embarrassed at the way this conversation was going.

'Rubbish,' replied his Lordship, 'You are a working artist and as the Bible says, 'A workman is worthy of his hire'. I looked at the prices on some of the others. Would you be agreeable to £500 for the two children's portraits and throw in that delicious little watercolour of the South front?'

'That was really only a quick sketch to work up into a painting.'

'Well, I love it and would rather have that so it can fit on the wall above my desk.'

Jade could hardly believe she would start her exhibition five hundred pounds up before anyone saw her paintings. The Maweses had hired a marquee for their annual summer party, and it came a week in advance so that Jade could display her work in there. She realised she was exceedingly fortunate to have two artists in the family. As the students from the art college in Birmingham were already on vacation her parents came with screens which they had borrowed. They also helped her display her work to best advantage. The plans to go ahead with the new use of Ambersleigh Hall as a part of Liverpool University had been agreed in principle, so it was decided that there were to be architects' drawings at the other end of the marquee from Jade's paintings. This meant even more people from the locality would want to come noseying around and would therefore give her a wider audience. All was going well, and Jade suddenly thought of Dave. Perhaps he would like to come and see how well she was doing. She phoned him, told him the date of the private view and how to get to Ambersleigh.

CHAPTER TWENTY-SEVEN

June the seventeenth was the day. The girls woke early, Jade with excitement, and Beth with the knowledge that she would have to do even more than usual, with so many visitors, so much catering and the children to look after on her own, while Jade and Lord and Lady Mawes wandered round the marquee making small talk and entertaining the visitors. She didn't really mind as she was so happy for her friend to have this wonderful opportunity to show her work.

She got up first and went to see to the children, while Jade had a shower and hair wash, and tried to make herself look like an artist. She twisted her hair, which was again at shoulder length, into a knot with a piece of twig threaded through it, attached to a green ribbon.

She had bought an emerald green smock in the local market and put this on over shiny black tights and dressed it all up with an assortment of multi-coloured beads and necklaces.

'Wow,' said Beth when she had finally dressed Alice and Charlie and given them breakfast,' You look stunning.'

'Thanks a bundle,' laughed Jade giving her best friend a huge hug

'Wish me luck'

'I don't need to,' said Beth, 'It's going to be amazing, the best day of your life. Who knows you might even meet the lover of your dreams looking like that? Don't worry about anything else. I shall bring the children in to see the paintings and then take them off for a long walk and a picnic. The weather is perfect; sunny but not too hot, so you won't swelter in the marquee'

Beth returned downstairs and Jade gave a twirl in the mirror, admiring the effect of the emerald green and the hair. She was so happy she realised it didn't matter if she sold any paintings or not. It was just going to be such a fun day. She almost ran down the huge oak staircase and grabbing a bun ran out to the marquee. All was ready and she was glad it was to be a morning and afternoon private view, not the traditional evening. Daylight was so much better for viewing her artwork. Lord and Lady Mawes were already out there. They were looking at the display of drawings which showed their beautiful old house as it would look if it became a College of Art, Architecture and Horticulture. The plans were still fluid, but they were taking shape, and however difficult the transition was going to be, it felt right. Their children would be brought up in the old family home, and they would still have a private entrance and a private garden. What is more they would be able to afford to do it all up, redecorate and replant and have a proper nanny and full-time gardener, without selling off or parting with any of the land. They held hands as they looked together at their future, which was now secure. Beth came in and the children ran around their parents' legs, laughing and playing. It was such a happy family scene, that Beth couldn't help feeling a twinge of envy. Would this ever happen for her, she wondered. The children recognised themselves in Jade's portraits of them asleep and had a good look at pictures of their house before Beth took them off for their picnic, carrying a big rug and a bag full of goodies which she had put together.

Meanwhile Jade was putting the finishing touches to her exhibition. She had decided to group her paintings into separate screens for portraits, pictures of the house, landscapes and her less figurative works. She had a portfolio of mounted but unframed pictures and had prepared a proper catalogue with the names of the paintings and the prices on it, so that visitors could view the works unhindered by any labels. Jade was more interested in people viewing her work than measuring up the cost. She was as interested in their opinions as in their money. She had set up a small table by the entrance to the marquee and would be able to welcome each visitor and hand out a sheet about her exhibition personally. It was warm, sunny and going to be such fun.

CHAPTER TWENTY-EIGHT

Dave woke up late. He had an incipient headache and half wondered whether to travel all that way to Ambersleigh Hall to see Jade and her exhibition. He roused himself on one elbow, looked at the clock, groaned and swung his feet out. He knew he ought to make the effort. Jade had been so kind to him since they'd met up again, and it really wasn't such a huge distance to travel. He wandered off to the bathroom, dosed himself up with a couple of paracetamols, and started to dress. He had a strange feeling of anxiety as he did this. It wasn't a big deal to go to an art exhibition, he didn't have to stay long and yet he felt a sense of dread and déjà vu. Perhaps he was coming down with something. The paracetamol was not yet working.

He dressed more carefully than usual, as he knew he would bump into Lord and Lady Mawes and that it was always best to make a good impression when meeting people for the first time, especially when those people had put work his way, through friends, at a time when he had needed it most. He was very grateful for that; had written to thank them and thought he would take a nice bunch of flowers with him for Lady Mawes and maybe for Jade too.

He shaved, brushed his hair and put on a tie with his blazer. The tie was gold, and the blazer a deep navy. He looked smart and business like, and yet he saw in the mirror that he really was unusually pale and when he turned away from the mirror, he felt giddy and nearly lost his balance.

He set off after a light breakfast feeling rougher by the minute. His headache was no longer incipient it was coming at him in waves. He felt hot and bothered but drove on and stopped to buy flowers at a garage. As he bent to choose them his neck felt uncomfortably stiff, and he was slightly nauseous. He nearly turned back, but said to himself 'don't be such a wimp' and carried on eventually finding Ambersleigh Hall and large signs pointing the way to the 'Exhibitions'.

As Dave approached the marquee, he could see Jade sitting in the entrance looking glamorous and arty. ' Good girl', he thought, and realised he really was 'over her' and just interested as a friend to see her paintings. He gave her a kiss on the cheek, and she shot to her feet with a huge grin and took him over to introduce him to Lord and Lady Mawes. There followed the usual polite conversations and Dave looked over the drawings of the Hall as it would become in the next few months and years. Jade had returned to her post at the entrance and Dave went to look at her paintings. He was beginning to feel decidedly ill by now and realised his fever had risen and his neck was stiffening up even more. Even so he gave Jade's pictures his full attention and realised what a talent she had. He had returned to the entrance of the marquee and was standing there just as two small children rushed in shouting,

'Mummy; Daddy. We saw an enormous bird down by the lake, this big, with a huge fish in its mouth'. Several visitors smiled at this lovely family intrusion into the tent. Then behind the children came a charming, sweet faced, happy looking girl, who was obviously the nanny.

'My God. It's Beth!' he thought:

Dave just stared in disbelief as Jade jumped up and said,

'O look. Here is my friend Beth, I've told you so much about. Do say hello and make yourselves known to each other. I have to go over there and speak to those people looking at my artwork.'

Beth and Dave just stood there transfixed. At length Beth spoke 'I didn't realise Jade's friend was you. She said his name was Dave and that he was a computer expert, but there must be hundreds of those in the country.'

She was trying to look normal, while inside there was a maelstrom of churning feelings at seeing him again. It was such a shock. She stood there unsure what she was either thinking or feeling. Suddenly Dave said,

'Excuse me,' and sat down abruptly on Jade's vacated chair. He was beginning to feel as if he might be hallucinating. His pulse was racing, and the headache was blinding him. He put his head in his hands and groaned.

'Nice to see you too,' said Beth sharply, and then realised that the man before her was not reacting emotionally or rationally but seemed genuinely ill. She went over to Lady Mawes and spoke to her.

'I wonder if someone else could keep an eye on the children for a while. There's a visitor by the entrance to the marquee who has been taken ill. I think I should get an ambulance for him.'

Lord Mawes looked across and saw Dave sitting in a heap by the table.

'That's very kind of you, Beth. We have lots of friends coming today with children and I know one of them would be only too happy to oblige. Jade is really up to her ears with prospective buyers and the housekeeper is engrossed in managing the caterers. If you're sure you can manage the visitor who's been taken ill, leave the children here in the marquee with us and don't worry. We'll be fine. They've had their picnic, haven't they?'

'Yes. I'm sure I shall be back soon,' said Beth in her calmest voice. She went back to Dave.

'Can you walk with me, and I'll get you some medical help.'

Dave nearly passed out as he left the marquee and Beth immediately dialled 111 on her mobile. She sort of knew already that Dave was seriously ill, but the paramedic said,' it sounds like meningitis. Can you get him to a hospital a.s.a.p.?'

She grabbed hold of his elbow and ushered him round the house to the family parking place, where she managed to bundle him into the car and drive off. He was rambling by now and saying 'Beth. I thought I saw Beth. I want to talk to her. Where are we? Where are we going? I must see Beth. I have to ask her about the baby. Don't lock me away. I'm not mad.'

'Shush,' said Beth, 'I'm taking you to Liverpool hospital. Close your eyes and try to rest.'

By the time she got there Dave was pouring with sweat and hardly coherent. He certainly didn't know Beth or respond to the medics in a rational way. They whisked him off upstairs on a trolley and Beth started to react. She suddenly felt very shaky indeed and a kind nurse brought her a cup of hot, sweet tea.

'Don't worry love. Your partner is in good hands, and they have caught this pretty early. We will let you know as soon as we can what treatment they will give him and whether he needs to stay in hospital. You may need to fetch some things for him.'

Beth burst into tears. She couldn't explain to this stranger that Dave wasn't her partner, but that he had been, that he had left her in the lurch and that he had more or less ruined her life. In the last half hour, she had relived over two years of emotional agony. She sat for two hours, by turns feeling angry, tearful, desolate and jinxed. How come after all these months that they should have to meet up again like this. She was just getting over that whole episode in the mental hospital and beginning to accept that she had lost her baby for ever, and then the architect of her misery was here, back in her life, and needing her to look after him. It wasn't fair.

Back at Ambersleigh Jade was blissfully unaware of what had happened. She saw that Beth and Dave had both left the marquee and assumed they were getting to know each other. The

Maweses were too busy talking to their visitors to tell Jade and anyway they didn't realise, since Beth had gone, just how ill the young man had been. The children were with friends and the art exhibition was arousing considerable interest. Jade had sold three paintings by lunchtime and many more people were expected in the afternoon.

All was well at Ambersleigh, and all was decidedly unwell at the Royal University hospital. Beth sat and sat, wondering why she was here and whether she should just ditch Dave and get back to her duties at Ambersleigh.

Something kept her here doggedly waiting for news. Maybe it was Dave's ramblings in the car about wanting to see Beth and talk to her. Maybe it was old stirrings of love. Maybe it was bloody-mindedness, so when he did recover, she could tell him what a bastard he'd been. She really didn't know, so she just sat.

Dave had been taken up to intensive care, but the hospital was too busy to let her know. Eventually the kind nurse returned.

'I'm afraid your husband is in intensive care. He won't be coming home for a few days, He has viral meningitis, and yes, it does strike incredibly quickly and can be very dangerous. You had better go home and leave us with a mobile number so we can contact you if we need to.'

'Thank you,' said Beth, rather forlornly, and having left her number she drove back slowly to Ambersleigh. The word husband had driven another dagger of pain into her, but she hadn't contradicted the nurse. Why not? Her head was spinning.

It was like being in a dream. When she got back the marquee was buzzing with people. Jade was whizzing around putting little red stickers on her sold paintings. The more she sold, the more people thought maybe they should get one while they still could. She was on a roller coaster and hardly noticed Beth's grave and pale looks. Beth, as usual, was putting a brave face on things, but she couldn't hold it all together for ever. After tea the marquee was closed, and it was bath and bedtime for Alice and Charlie. Lord and Lady Mawes were off out for a social function and the house settled back to some semblance of normality. Jade totted up how much money she had made and was astonished to find that all but three of her paintings had sold. She had made over £3000 in the afternoon including the sale to Lord Mawes of the children's portraits. She sank into a comfy chair and finally looked at Beth properly.

'Are you OK?' she asked, somewhat surprised to see that although it had been the best day of her life, for Beth it seemed to have been anything but.

'You don't look right at all. What's happened?'

'I don't know where to begin,' said Beth, and the tears started to fall. Jade gave her a huge hug and said,

'Why not start at the beginning and I'll just listen and try not to interrupt'

So, Beth started and it took half an hour to explain her life up until that moment. She didn't omit anything. She told her friend all about the love affair, the pregnancy, the abortion and the incarceration in the mental hospital. She explained how she couldn't have imagined they both knew the same Dave, and what a shock it had been to see him there in the marquee, and then the suddenness of his collapse and the awful feelings she'd had when she realised he had a life-threatening form of meningitis.

It all poured out and Jade sat there, stunned and alarmed at the state of her friend. She had never before seen her so emotional and the story she was telling was totally unlike the calm and buttoned up Beth she had known for nearly a year.

When the flood subsided Beth realised that though she felt wrung out she also felt better for having told the truth, not only to her friend but to herself. In spite of everything she was better. She was more confident in herself. She did have a wonderful job with lovely employers, and she did in fact still love Dave, even after all he had put her through; the thought of finding him again and then losing him so quickly had focussed her mind on how exactly she felt about him. What on earth should she do?

CHAPTER TWENTY-NINE

Dave came round in a high iron bed, attached to drips and wires and feeling incredibly thirsty. He was still running a high fever, but the nurses near him seemed to think he was out of danger. He could hear their mutterings as if from some distance away. 'We'd better inform his wife that he will be back on a ward soon,' they said as Dave struggled to remember where he was and why. He knew he had nearly died. He remembered that feeling very briefly of floating above his body and looking down from a corner of the room while people worked on his body, which was no longer his. He wished he could remember more, but there again he was glad to think he was actually alive, even though he was beginning to realise it was a different him. For a start they kept calling him David, a name no one had used since he was four years old. Then again, this talk of a wife was strange. He didn't know he had one. Later that day they came and removed the attachments and said he was able to eat something. He had little appetite and even holding a spoonful of soup to his mouth seemed like a huge effort. He was so weak that he fell back exhausted and wondered when he would regain his strength. Eventually a doctor came and examined him.

'You've had a near miss my boy,' said the young man who looked no older than himself. 'We will keep you under observation for three days on a ward. We need the ICU beds for people coming in like you near death's door. Don't try and get up. They will wheel you down on a trolley. Make sure you take things slowly. The recuperation can take several weeks when you've had this sort of meningitis. Can you go somewhere to rest and be looked after?'

'O yes thanks. I have a wife.' 'Apparently' he added under his breath.

The hospital corridors they wheeled him down seemed endless and he lay back exhausted by the lights and the noises round him. On the ward he was given curtains round his bed and almost immediately fell asleep.

It was when he heard other voices in the room that he realised it was visiting time. He closed his eyes and didn't see the person who crept in and sat quietly next to his bed. But he was really only dozing and when he turned and half opened his eyes there sat Jade, looking much more ordinary now in jeans and sweatshirt with her reddish hair loose on her shoulders

'Hi there Dave. You've given us all an awful fright. Not to mention a certain person an awful shock.'

'Are you my wife?' he asked, confused as to what she was doing there.

'Good Lord, no. Whatever made you think that?'

'Well, they told me upstairs they were going to tell my wife I was coming back on a ward.'

'That was Beth's only way of gaining access to you up in the intensive care unit. We don't have any details about where your parents are, so we couldn't let them know how life threatening your illness was. Beth wasn't prepared to see you up there, struggling for life all alone, and so she let them think you two were married so they would let her in to sit by your bedside. When you're well enough I am going to give you such an ear-wigging as you've never had before, about the way you've treated that poor creature. In fact, I'll start now. She is the nicest, kindest, sweetest person I have ever met and you, you…'

Fortunately for Dave a bell rang to announce the end of visiting times and Jade had to get up.

'Don't think I'm bringing you grapes and things,' she said as she leant over and kissed him on the forehead, 'I'll be back.'

With that she was gone and left Dave there utterly exhausted and confused as to how his old flame and his ex-love had met up and seemed to be together. It was a bizarre world and being so ill had made it all seem even more unreal.

CHAPTER THIRTY

Dave's parents came after three days, and his mother could hardly stop herself from crying all the time. It had been months since they'd seen their darling only son. He had drifted away gradually through his university years, and they had accepted this as part of his growing up, but this last year, when he had been abroad for much of the time, there had been little real contact. They were shocked at how thin he was, and how near death he had been. His father sat quietly by the bedside while mother fussed around. After a while he asked,

'Well, are you coming back with us to recuperate or what? Your old bedroom is still there, and we'd be happy to see you till you're better but we have quite a busy lifestyle in our retirement and we're out quite a bit.'

'Oh, Francis, how can you talk like that when we've got our boy back from the dead. Of course he must come home. Of course our 'lifestyle' isn't as important as having him home and feeding him up and looking after him till he's really well again.'

'Hang on,' said Dave, 'I need to do something before I go anywhere. I was brought here, hallucinating, by a young woman called Beth. She sat by my bedside in intensive care and has looked after me till I came back to my senses, and I haven't seen her since. I must thank her properly before I leave here. I might not have another chance.'

'Well of course,' said his parents. It would be another twenty-four hours before he was discharged and they said they would return for him then and give him time to sort himself out.

Dave tried to find a way to contact Beth, but he had no number and Jade was simply not answering her phone. In the end, in desperation, he rang Ambersleigh Hall and asked to speak to Lord Mawes. He was put through and explained that he was the young man they had helped to find work and who had fallen ill in their marquee. He asked if he could speak to Beth, but there was a hesitation in His Lordship's manner. After a few moments he spoke.

'Look here, young man, we have the highest regard for Beth. She has been a tower of strength to us and absolutely wonderful with our children. Ever since you came on the scene she hasn't been eating properly. She's looking very fragile and I'm not sure seeing you again would be in her best interests. We will pass on your thanks to her.'

He was about to put down the receiver when Dave suddenly said 'Please give her a message. Say I want to marry her.'

'Marry her? You hardly know the girl. What on earth are you talking about?'

'But I do know her,' said Dave,' I love her very dearly, only I didn't realise it till just recently. I let her down very badly over a year ago and now I want to make amends. Please, please tell her.'

He put the phone down and lay back exhausted on the pillow. He was near to tears as he thought how his feelings for Beth, so selfish in the past, had blossomed into this all-encompassing love for her. Could she ever forgive him? Could she ever possibly love him as she once had?

That evening at visiting time he waited on tenterhooks to see if she would come, and when she didn't, he realised that his hope was stupid and any good fortune would be entirely undeserved. He thought of how he had reacted when she told him she was pregnant. He blushed to himself remembering his suggesting they get rid of their baby. He had hurt Beth more than any other human being. She deserved better than him. When he'd seen her at the door of the marquee, she'd looked happy, serene, bright eyed and beautiful. Now, according to Lord Mawes she was fretting and unwell. It was all his fault.

He lay back once more and closed his eyes. It was five minutes till the end of visiting time and people were leaving. As he drifted into a light sleep, he felt a small hand slip into his. It was warm and strangely familiar

'Yes,' said a soft voice, 'yes. I will.'

CHAPTER THIRTY-ONE

The end of the month was approaching. September had been dry and warm and the countryside round Liverpool had seemed extraordinarily beautiful. Lord and Lady Mawes had formally signed the house over to the University. Builders were already coming in to brick up passageways between the private wing and what was to be University accommodation. Jade had applied to be the first Art student to live there when it was completed. Meanwhile she was invited to stay on in her old bedroom. Beth had been given a fortnight's paid holiday and compassionate leave and had taken Dave to a health spa where they both could recuperate and build up their strength. They had so much history to share, so many moments of joy and pain and a lifetime to look forward to together which would never be clouded by lies or deceit. They were sad about the baby that they would never see, but Beth insisted that it would be unkind and unfair to the couple who had adopted her to seek her out and try to get her back. She knew the heartache of longing for a child and there was no reason why she should not have another or several, whereas the adoptive parents had been trying for ten years to conceive. She had been told that in the hospital when she had signed the papers.

It all seemed a very long time ago, she thought as she nestled her head between Dave's head and shoulder and burrowed into him like a young lamb. She couldn't believe how he had changed in the months they had been apart. She had always loved his looks, his fun and his intelligence. Now she was experiencing a kindness and concern that filled her with satisfaction and happiness. He had grown up and matured into a fine man. They visited his parents, who were delighted with their daughter–in-law to be and the thought of eventually becoming grandparents.

Alice and Charlie were less delighted.

'Are you going away then and leaving us?' questioned Alice, and Charlie stamped his foot in a puddle and said,

'No. Naughty Beth. Can't go away. No'

Lord and Lady Mawes called her in one evening to their sitting room.

'Please sit down Beth. We want to talk to you. We are so pleased to see you so happy and well. We think your Dave is just right for you and we would be the first to understand that you need to make a new life together, but we are devastated at the thought of going back to the way life was before you came here. You and Jade have made such a difference. We will have a smaller house and people looking after the grounds, but might you consider staying on as nanny until Charlie is at least of school age. We can let you have a cottage in the grounds. It has been empty for three years and needs modernising, but we can afford to do all sorts of things now. Dave could commute easily to Liverpool from here and we would offer it to you both rent free as well as paying you a proper nanny's salary. What do you think?'

Beth stuttered her thanks and went to discuss this with Dave, but there was no need to consider the proposal. It was perfect and would enable them to have a wonderful start to married life. They had been offered the use of the Hall for the reception and there was no need to wait. They could go ahead and marry and be in situ for the next Christmas.

All of the parents would be invited, along with the Mawes family, and Alice and Charlie would be bridesmaid and page boy.

Jenny was invited up from the Dover Sally Army hostel and there were a few friends but it was quite a small ceremony, which was what Dave and Beth wanted.

Jade came, looking rather sheepish, with a young man in tow. She had met him at her exhibition just as Beth had said she would.